Once upon a time there were two little angels called Bel and Bub.

One was very good . . .

. . . some of the time.

One was very bad . . .

. . . some of the time.

But most of the time they
were a little bit of both.

Jan Pieńkowski

Bel and Bub
and the Big Brown Box

A Dorling Kindersley Book

Wham!

One day Bel and Bub had
a surprise. A big brown box
arrived out of the blue.

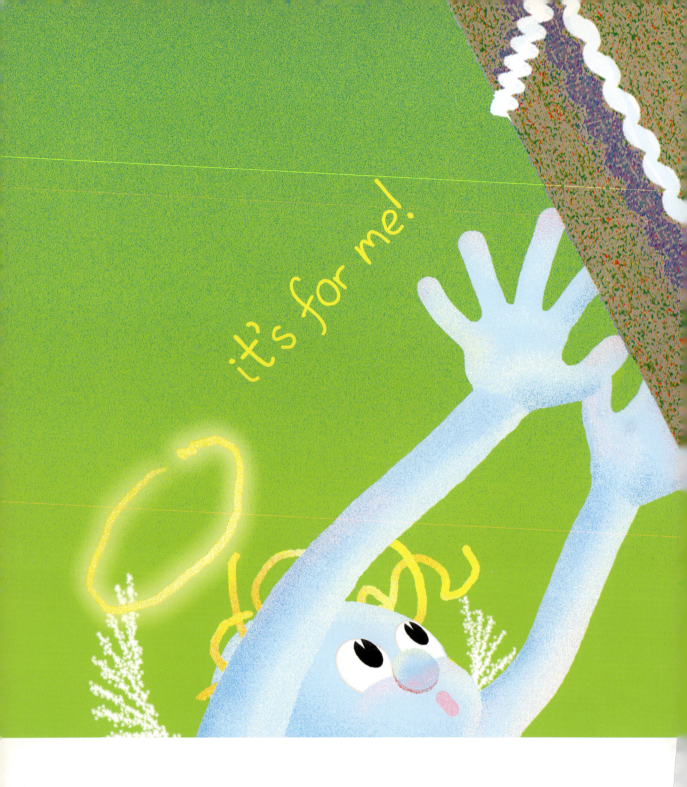

Bel thought the package was for her.

Bub thought it was for him.

it's big

They brought the package
home and tore it open.

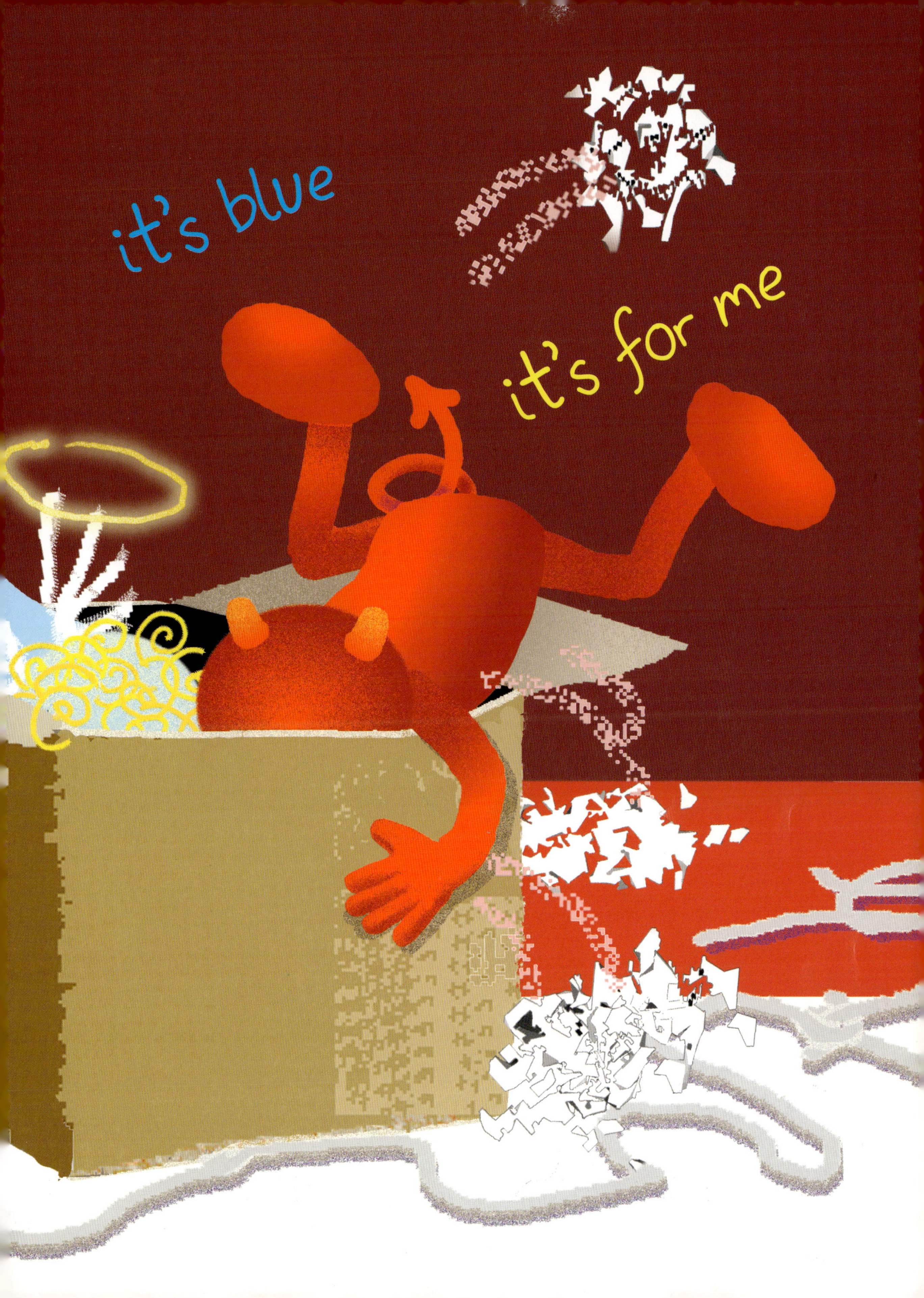
it's blue
it's for me

Inside were two brand
new T-shirts.

One was yellow and one
was blue. Bel didn't like hers.

thump

THERE WAS TROUBLE !

Now there were two torn T-shirts.

There were also
some yellow scraps of cloth
and lots of blue scraps.

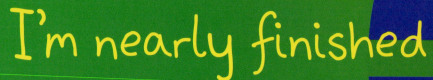

I'm nearly finished

Bel and Bub patched things up just in time.

They showed how they had shared their presents.

Then they got a
special treat.

Bub had strawberry.
Bel had vanilla.

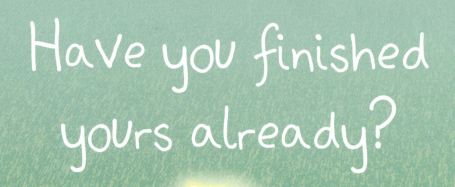

Have you finished
yours already?